For Mom & Dad, who showed me the stars and how to work hard to reach them.

DIAL BOOKS FOR YOUNG READERS
An imprint of Penguin Random House LLC, New York

First published in the United States of America by Dial Books for Young Readers, an imprint of Penguin Random House LLC, 2022

Dial & colophon are registered trademarks of Penguin Random House LLC. Visit us online at penguinrandomhouse.com.
Library of Congress Cataloging-in-Publication Data is available. Manufactured in China • ISBN 9780593324387

10 9 8 7 6 5 4 3 2 1
HH

Design by Jennifer Kelly
Text handlettered by Vanessa Roeder

The art for this book was created with acrylic paint, collaged paper, colored pencils, and assembled digitally.

THE STACK

Vanessa Roeder

Dial Books for Young Readers

It started with a single chair.

On it, Luna reached
up high...

But couldn't quite
get there.

Even with a stepping stool
it was a tad too low.

She ran away and then returned
with twenty books in tow.

Luna stacked them,
ONE
BY
ONE,
with vigilance and care,

and when she climbed atop the stack
she started to despair.

Her quest seemed insurmountable.
She had to think much bigger.

She planned
a complicated
scheme
to execute
with vigor.

Atop the books
she placed her bed,
set upright
on its end.

Next she tossed a clawfoot tub that held her tallest friend.

Luna piled on
stacks of plates,
Her mother's
finest set.

Then

she launched

her neighbor's

house.

Did you hear something?

I think the squirrels are back.

But she couldn't reach just yet.

An elephant,

a humpback whale,

her grandpa's station wagon . . .

I don't trust this newfangled GPS system.

TURN LEFT AT THE ELEPHANT

She flung
a princess in
a tower...

REROUTING...

I don't
think it's
squirrels.

WHOA.

She even chucked the dragon.

FINALLY atop
the beast
she heaved a
pirate ship.

Trixie, I have a
feeling we're not
at Grandma's
anymore.

She grabbed a pack,
a jar, a snack
and started
on her trip.

She climbed and clambered

up she went

with all her strength and might.

cucumber?

up to
its highest
height.

She scaled the great
colossal stack

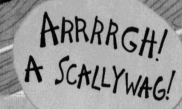

ARRRRGH!
A SCALLYWAG!

You're
not a
prince.

Carefully she
perched on top and
opened up the jar.

Luna stood on tippy-toe to reach a single star.

She placed the twinkling star inside and screwed the lid on tight.

With
the
prize

clutched
in her
arms

she
made
her
downward
flight.

Back inside her room that night
the gleaming starlight spread.

She glanced
around her room
and wished…

she hadn't tossed her bed.

TURN LEFT AT THE ELEPHANT

But Luna didn't mind so much.

She had her
light instead.